THE TREASURE TROOP

The Hidden Room

by Dori Hillestad Butler

illustrated by Tim Budgen

Penguin Workshop

For Ben and Andy–DHB

For Julia–TB

PENGUIN WORKSHOP
An Imprint of Penguin Random House LLC, New York

Text copyright © 2021 by Dori Hillestad Butler. Illustrations copyright © 2021 by Penguin Random House LLC. All rights reserved. Published by Penguin Workshop, an imprint of Penguin Random House LLC, New York. PENGUIN and PENGUIN WORKSHOP are trademarks of Penguin Books Ltd, and the W colophon is a registered trademark of Penguin Random House LLC. Printed in the USA.

Visit us online at www.penguinrandomhouse.com.

Library of Congress Cataloging-in-Publication Data
is available upon request.

ISBN 9780593094853 (pbk)
ISBN 9780593094860 (hc)

10 9 8 7 6 5 4 3 2 1
10 9 8 7 6 5 4 3 2 1

Chapter 1

A NEW ENVELOPE

"Marly Deaver, you've got mail!" Marly's older brother Nick dropped a blue envelope with her name on it onto the kitchen table.

Marly was still half asleep. She yawned and rubbed her unpatched eye beneath her glasses. Though she was almost nine years old, she *still* had to wear a patch to train her bad eye to work as well as her good eye.

She reached for the envelope, but her other brother, Noah, grabbed it first.

"Hey!" Marly cried as Noah held the envelope out of her reach.

"This better not be another letter about a will," Noah grumbled, trying to read it through the envelope.

2

A few weeks ago, Marly had received a letter inviting her to the reading of Harry Summerling's will. Mr. Summerling was the Deavers' next-door neighbor. Unfortunately, he had died earlier in the summer. Marly still couldn't believe she was never going to see him again.

But he had left something in his will for Marly and two other kids in her grade—Isla Thomson and Sai Gupta. A treasure hunt! Hunting for treasure had been Mr. Summerling's favorite thing in the world. In fact, he'd died while hunting for treasure off the coast of Washington State.

Marly, Isla, and Sai didn't know each other very well before Mr. Summerling's treasure hunt. But they had become good friends while working together on all the puzzles. The treasure turned out to be a secret tree house hidden in the woods behind Mr. Summerling's and Marly's houses.

Marly hopped up and snatched the envelope from Noah's hands. "I hope you know it's a crime to steal someone else's mail," she said. "Where'd you find this, anyway?" It just had her name on it. No address. So it couldn't have come through the post office.

"Under the mat on the front porch," Nick replied. He and Noah had been going out for early morning runs because they hoped to make the eighth-grade cross-country team when school started in a couple of weeks.

Marly tore open the envelope and pulled out a sheet of paper. It read:

me etm eat thetre ehou seat
on eocl ockto day
weha vestu ffto tal kab out
yo urfri end
SG

Marly felt a thrill of excitement. The letter was in code!

"Well?" Nick asked as he pulled out a chair beside Marly. "What is it? Who's it from?"

Marly didn't answer. But she was pretty sure *SG* was Sai Gupta.

Noah peered over Marly's other shoulder. "Can't tell. It's in code."

Marly clasped the paper to her chest and glared at her brothers.

"Marly must be involved in something pretty shady if she and her friends have to talk in code," Nick said.

Noah nodded. "What are you involved in, little sister?"

"Boys!" Mom said in a warning voice.

"Stop teasing your sister," Dad chimed in.

Nick held up his hands in surrender. Noah sat down between Nick and Dad. While the rest of the family got their breakfast and talked among themselves, Marly hunched over her letter.

Before Mr. Summerling's treasure hunt, Marly had had no idea how much fun it was to solve puzzles and codes. Or that she was actually good at it. But she was.

Even with her eye patch on, it didn't take her long to crack Sai's code. The third line practically gave it away. All the spaces between the "words" were in the wrong places.

Feeling a sense of accomplishment, Marly mentally moved the spaces until she had the whole message decoded:

meet me at the tree house at
one o clock today
we have stuff to talk about
your friend
SG

"Mom?" She lifted her head. "Can I go to the tree house this afternoon at one o'clock?"

"By yourself?"

"We'll go with her," Noah offered.

"Yeah. We want to see this tree house," Nick put in.

Marly ignored them. "I won't be alone," she said. "Isla and Sai will be there, too."

"Yes, you can go," Mom said.

"Yay!" Marly grinned. She wondered what Sai wanted to talk about.

Tall fences separated Marly's and Mr. Summerling's yards from the woods, so Marly entered the woods at the end of her street. She and her new friends had needed GPS coordinates to find the tree house the first time. But now they'd been there often enough that they all knew the way.

Dried sticks and leaves crunched beneath Marly's feet. As she passed the tree with the two trunks braided together, she began scanning tree branches for the tiny wooden house. There it was!

She hurried around to the other side of the tree, climbed the rope ladder, and spun the dials on the lock to 1-5-3. The little half door swung open and she crawled inside the house.

Isla sat perched on a tree stump stool with a game of solitaire spread out on the table in front of her. Sai was nowhere in sight.

"I was wondering when you guys would get here," Isla said, adjusting her headband. Isla always wore a headband with cat ears on it. Today's was turquoise.

"Where's Sai?" Marly asked, rising to her feet.

Isla shrugged. "Haven't seen him yet."

Weird, Marly thought, considering he was the one who'd called this meeting. She went

to the window and peered out over the forest. Unfortunately, everything looked blurry. She tried sliding her patch onto the temple of her glasses, but that didn't help.

Marly turned to Isla. "Do you know what he wants to talk about?"

Isla shook her head. "Wanna play a game while we wait?"

"Sure." Marly slid her patch back where it belonged and joined Isla at the table.

"How about crazy eights?" Isla gathered up her solitaire game, reshuffled the cards, and dealt them out.

A few minutes later, Marly heard a noise at the door. She turned as it swung open.

Sai crawled into the tree house. "Sorry I'm late," he said. "I had to stay after summer school."

"How come?" Isla asked.

Sai wrinkled his nose. "I don't want to talk about it." He reached into his front pocket and pulled out a mini flashlight. "Let's talk about this instead!"

"A flashlight?" Marly said.

"No. Not a flashlight." Sai turned it on with his thumb and the light cast a bluish glow onto the table. "It's a black light. My dad uses it to make sure the money in our cash register isn't counterfeit."

Sai's family owned a convenience store a few blocks away.

"Why did you bring it here?" Isla asked.

Sai grinned. "I'm glad you asked. Remember

that box we found under there?" He aimed his light at the red rug in the middle of the floor.

"Yeah," Marly said slowly. How could any of them forget the metal box they'd found hidden beneath the floorboards under that rug? There wasn't much in it, though. Just a note inviting them to use it to hide their own treasures, and a few unused pieces of paper *From the Desk of Harry P. Summerling.*

"Did you ever wonder why there were blank papers in that box?" Sai asked.

Marly hadn't. And she could tell by the look on Isla's face that she hadn't, either.

"I figured they're just leftover papers from when Mr. Summerling made up all those codes for our treasure hunt," Isla said.

"Maybe," Sai said mysteriously. "But what if those papers aren't really blank? What if there's something written on them in invisible ink?"

Chapter 2

HIDDEN MESSAGES

"Really, Sai?" Marly resisted the urge to roll her eyes. "Invisible ink?"

Isla adjusted her headband. "Why would you think there'd be another message tucked away in that box?"

"I don't know," Sai said, avoiding their gaze. "It doesn't hurt to look, does it?" He started rolling up the red carpet in the middle of the room.

Marly and Isla exchanged doubtful looks. "I guess not," Isla said.

13

The girls helped Sai finish rolling. But secretly, Marly thought Sai probably just wanted an excuse to play with his dad's black light.

"All right," Marly said. "Where's the T?"

That was how they'd discovered the secret compartment to begin with. The letter they'd found at the end of the treasure hunt contained a secret message that told them to *make a T*, which meant they had to figure out where imaginary lines between the pictures on the tree house walls would meet. The secret compartment was right below that spot.

Sai stretched his arms out to the sides and lined up pictures of the flowers and the teddy bear. Then he turned sideways, took a few steps to the left, and lined up pictures of the globe and the telephone. "Right here," he said, stomping his foot.

They all crouched down and worked together to pry the loose boards from the

floor. As soon as they uncovered the blue
metal box, Sai pulled it up. He opened the lid
and shined his black light on the top paper
From the Desk of Harry P. Summerling.

"It's blank," Isla said.

"Big surprise," Marly muttered under her breath.

Sai set that paper aside and shined his light on the next one. That one was blank, too. So was the third paper. But when he shined his light on the fourth paper, letters appeared.

They all leaned in and gasped. There, on what used to be a blank page, was a word search puzzle.

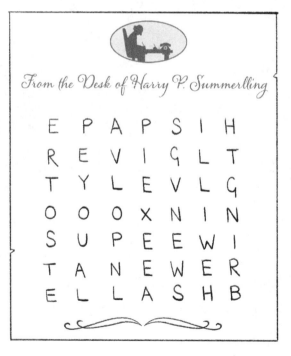

From the Desk of Harry P. Summerling

E P A P S I H
R E V I G L T
T Y L E V L G
O O O X N I N
S U P E E W I
T A N E W E R
E L L A S H B

"I knew it!" Sai raised his fist in the air.

Marly stared in amazement. Sai had been right about the invisible ink.

Isla's eyebrows scrunched together. "I don't get it."

"What don't you get?" Sai sat back on his heels. "It's a word search. That means there are words hidden—"

Isla raised her hand in protest. "I know what a word search is," she said. "What I don't know is *why* is there a word search puzzle written in invisible ink and hidden in that box?"

Marly nodded. "We finished the treasure hunt," she said as she stood up. "The last letter we found said so." She went to get her old third-grade science notebook, which was lying on top of the shelf of board games. They had used leftover pages from that notebook to solve Mr. Summerling's puzzles. And all the papers with the original puzzles were still tucked inside that notebook.

Marly riffled through the papers until she found the one she was looking for. "Aha!" she said, pulling it out. "Let me read it to you. 'Congratulations to my treasure troop! You've worked hard, and now you've come to the *end* of this treasure hunt—'"

"*This* treasure hunt," Sai interrupted, changing the emphasis. "That means there's *another* treasure hunt. And this"—he waved the paper with the word search in the air—"must be our first puzzle!"

"What?" Isla said. "Why would there be another treasure hunt?"

"Duh. Probably because there's more treasure," Sai said.

More treasure? Marly thought. *Is that possible?*

Though Mr. Summerling had traveled the world searching for buried treasure, no one knew whether he had ever found any. His son,

Jay, said he hadn't. Jay had been there for the reading of Mr. Summerling's will, too. Marly remembered how awkward that had felt. In his will, Mr. Summerling said Jay had been a terrible son who didn't deserve any treasure. That's why he left it all to Marly, Isla, and Sai. They had treated him much kinder than his own son had. But Jay didn't really care about that because he didn't think there was any treasure. That's why no one was surprised when the "treasure" turned out to be a tree house.

But what if there is more *treasure?*

"Well, why don't we do the puzzle and see if that gives us any new clues?" Marly suggested.

"Okay," Isla said, flipping her hair behind her shoulder.

They all sat down at the table and Sai shined his black light onto the paper to make the word search puzzle appear again.

"Maybe we should copy it into our notebook so you don't wear down the battery in your light," Marly suggested.

"Good idea," Sai said.

Marly dug a pencil out of her tote bag. Then Isla and Sai read lines from the puzzle out loud while Marly copied them into her notebook. When she finished, they all crowded together.

"Okay, what words do you guys see?" Marly asked. "I see *new*." She circled it.

"*Lash,*" Isla said. Marly circled that word, too.

"*Sup!*" Sai pointed at the *S U P*.

Isla laughed. "That's not a word."

"It is, too," Sai argued. "It means 'what's up?'"

"It could also mean supper," Marly said. "I say it counts."

Isla didn't look convinced, but Marly circled it anyway. "Here's another." Marly circled *R I N G*.

"And *bring*." Isla touched the *B* below the *R.*

Marly circled them both, but as her pencil followed the *I-N-G*, she noticed something else. "Wait a minute . . ." She continued her line up along the right-hand edge of the puzzle, then backward along the top.

"Oh, I see," Isla said, twisting her hair around her finger.

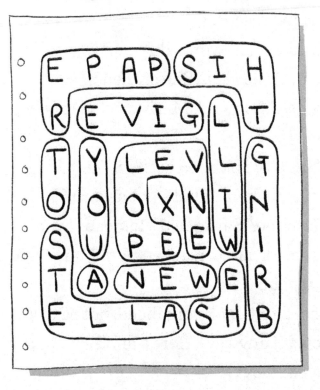

"What?" Sai leaned in. "What do you see?"

"It's not a word search. It's a message written in a puzzle that *looks* like a word search." Marly brought her pencil back to the *B* at the bottom right corner and traced the words as she read them out loud. "Bring . . . This . . . Paper . . ."

Now Sai saw it, too. He read along with Marly. "To . . . Stella . . . She . . . Will . . . Give . . . You . . . A . . . New . . . Envelope!"

Stella was Stella Lovelace, Mr. Summerling's attorney. She was the one who had sent them letters inviting them to the reading of Mr. Summerling's will.

"It *is* a whole new treasure hunt," Isla cried.

"Told you!" Sai said, hopping to his feet. "Time to pay Ms. Lovelace a visit!"

Chapter 3

MORE TREASURE

M s. Lovelace's office was located in a small brick building in downtown Sandford. A little sign out front read: Stella Lovelace, Attorney at Law. Marly, Isla, and Sai walked inside, and a lady behind the counter lifted her head.

Marly cleared her throat. "We're here to see Ms. Lovelace," she said politely.

"I'm sorry. Ms. Lovelace isn't available right now," the lady said, avoiding Marly's eye. Marly was used to that. Grown-ups never liked to make eye contact with kids who wore eye patches.

"That's okay. We'll wait." Sai drummed his hands on the counter.

"There are some chairs over here." Isla pointed.

The lady stood up. "You can't wait," she said. "Ms. Lovelace is going to be tied up all afternoon. But if you'd like to make an appointment—" Before she got the whole sentence out, a door opened behind her.

"What's going on?" Ms. Lovelace poked her head out. "Oh." Her face softened when she noticed Marly, Isla, and Sai.

"We brought you something," Sai said. "Show her, Marly."

Marly opened their notebook, turned to the latest puzzle, and held it up. "This says you have an envelope for us."

Ms. Lovelace smiled. "I sure do," she said. "Be right back." She closed her office door.

Less than a minute later, she returned with a plain white envelope and a flashlight. "Here you go!" She handed them to Isla.

"Thanks," Isla said, staring curiously at the flashlight.

"What's the flashlight for?" Sai asked.

Ms. Lovelace offered a tight-lipped smile and went back inside her office.

"Guess that's up to us to figure out," Marly said. "Come on, let's go."

But they couldn't wait until they got back to the tree house to find out what was inside the envelope. They hurried over to an open bench at the end of the street.

Isla set the flashlight between her and Sai, and tore open the envelope. Sai immediately grabbed the flashlight and started turning it on and off, on and off, on and off.

"Don't," Marly said, laying her hand over Sai's. "It looks like you're flashing SOS. People are going to think you need help!"

"Nuh-uh," Sai argued. "SOS is like this." He blinked short-short-short, long-long-long, short-short-short. "I'm doing this." He blinked on, off, on, off. "It's different."

Marly rolled her eyes.

"Do you want to hear our new letter?" Isla asked, holding up another paper *From the Desk of Harry P. Summerling*.

"Yes! Duh!" Marly and Sai spoke at the same time.

Isla smoothed the paper on her lap and began reading. "'Dear Treasure Troop. If you're reading this letter, that means you have found the tree house—'"

"Because we rock!" Sai interrupted.

"'You've also found the hidden cubbyhole inside the tree house,'" Isla continued. "'And you even found a way to read my invisible ink. Clearly, I have not underestimated you three at all.'"

"No, you have not," Sai said proudly.

Marly elbowed him. "Let her finish."

"'Guess what?'" Isla read. "'There is more treasure to be found!'" They all glanced at one another, their eyes shining with anticipation. "'You'll find what you need inside my house, in a hidden room that looks out over the city. But finding that room won't be easy. One ghost guards the doors. Another keeps the key. The very important key. I hope you're not afraid of ghosts.'" Isla swallowed hard, then kept reading. "'You have until August 25 to find the hidden room. Otherwise this treasure will be lost forever. If you ever find yourselves stuck, remember who you are. That will always get you through. Good luck! Yours, Harry P. Summerling.'"

"I can't believe it," Marly said. "There really is more treasure."

"And we get to go search a haunted house to find it," Sai said, rubbing his hands together.

A flash of concern crossed Isla's face when Sai said *haunted*. But she blinked it away. "I wonder what the treasure is," she said.

"I bet *this* time it'll be money," Sai said. They had all thought the treasure was going to be money last time. Marly had planned to use her share to buy a plane ticket to visit her friend Aubrey, who had moved away at the beginning of the summer. But she wasn't disappointed when it wasn't money. She still missed Aubrey, but she wasn't as lonely as she had been at the beginning of the summer. Not since she, Isla, and Sai had started spending time together.

Sai hopped down from the bench. "So, what's our next puzzle?" he asked eagerly.

"There isn't one," Isla said.

"What do you mean there isn't one?" Marly asked. There was always another puzzle.

Isla studied the paper. "We have to find a hidden room. That's all it says."

"Yeah, but we'll find it by solving a bunch of puzzles, right?" Sai said. "Like how we found the tree house."

"I don't know." Isla turned the paper over. It was blank on the other side. "I don't see any other puzzles."

"Maybe Ms. Lovelace was supposed to give us another envelope, too," Sai suggested.

That was how it had worked the first time. Ms. Lovelace had read that first letter from Mr. Summerling out loud. Then she gave them another envelope, which held their first puzzle.

"Let's go ask her!" Marly said, getting up from the bench.

Isla handed the letter to Marly, who shoved it inside her bag with the notebook. Then they marched back to Ms. Lovelace's office.

They opened the door and found

Ms. Lovelace standing at the front counter, riffling through some papers inside an open folder in front of her. She quickly closed it. "Yes?" she asked with an awkward smile as Marly, Isla, and Sai approached the counter.

They all nudged one another, trying to figure out who should do the talking. Marly decided she would. "Did you maybe forget to give us another envelope?" she asked boldly. "One that has another puzzle in it?"

"No," Ms. Lovelace said, running a hand through her hair. "I've given you everything I was supposed to give you."

"Are you sure?" Sai asked.

"Positive," Ms. Lovelace said.

Marly, Isla, and Sai exchanged surprised looks. *Now what?*

"Okay, thanks," Marly said. There was nothing else to do but leave.

"So . . . ," Isla said as they started down the street. "We're just supposed to go over to Mr. Summerling's house and look for a hidden room?"

"I guess?" Marly said. Though it seemed odd to her that they would have free rein to run around inside someone else's house all by themselves. Would their parents even allow that?

"If that's what the letter says, then that's what we have to do," Sai said, picking up the pace.

Marly agreed. Odd or not, they had to find the hidden room inside Mr. Summerling's house. They had to find the new treasure.

"Wait." Isla stopped walking. "How are we going to get inside the house?"

Marly stopped, too. "Good question," she said, scratching her head. They had a key to the gate to Mr. Summerling's front walk. They'd found it during the other treasure hunt. But they didn't have a key to his house. How *would* they get in?

"We'll figure it out when we get there," Sai said impatiently. "Come on!"

Marly and Isla raised eyebrows at each other. Finally, Marly shrugged. Maybe they would figure it out when they got there.

"Okay, but let's stop at Marly's house and tell our parents where we're going first," Isla said.

"Fine," Sai said.

They started walking again. But after a few steps, Marly suddenly had the strangest feeling someone was watching them. She turned and saw a mom pushing a little kid in a stroller, and two men in business suits carrying cups of coffee. None of them seemed to be paying any attention to the three of them.

They kept going. But still, Marly couldn't shake that feeling. Nor could she stop glancing over her shoulder.

"What's the matter, Marly?" Isla asked the third time she did it. "Why do you keep turning around?"

"I don't know," Marly said. "I just have this weird feeling that someone's watching us."

"Who?" Isla asked.

"I don't know," Marly said again.

Sai turned all the way around. "I don't see anyone."

"Neither do I," Isla said.

Marly knew Isla and Sai both had way better eyes than she did. If they didn't see anyone, then there probably wasn't anyone there.

"Let's just go," she said.

Chapter 4

LOCKED UP

"You want to *what*?" Marly's mom leaned back in her desk chair, her eyes fixed on Marly and her friends. "No. Absolutely not. You are not going to wander around inside Mr. Summerling's house by yourselves."

Marly half expected this. "But he wants us to. See?" She showed her mother the letter Ms. Lovelace had given them, then held her breath while Mom read it to herself.

Isla and Sai shuffled their feet and avoided looking at Marly's mom. They all knew that if

they could get one parent to agree to this, the others would probably agree, too.

"I don't know, honey . . ." Mom handed the letter back to Marly.

"You always said Mr. Summerling was quirky," Marly said. "You said he was quirky, but nice. This is just another example of him being quirky!"

Mom tilted her head. That meant she was thinking about it.

"Please, Mom," Marly begged.

"Please, Mrs. Deaver!" Isla and Sai chimed in.

Mom sighed. "Why don't you all get yourselves a snack while I talk to the other parents and see what they think," she said, reaching for the phone on her desk.

The kids went into the kitchen, and Marly got everyone cartons of yogurt. They ate standing up.

"Our parents are never going to let us do this," Isla said.

"They might," Sai said.

Marly didn't say anything. But now that they knew there was more treasure to be found, their parents had to let them search. They just had to!

As they were finishing their yogurt, Marly's mom came in. "Two hours," she said. "I want you all back here in two hours. And be respectful while you're there."

The kids all jumped up and slapped high fives.

"Thanks, Mom!" Marly gave her mom a hug. Then she and her friends trooped next door.

A tall hedge and black wrought iron fence surrounded Mr. Summerling's property. There were old appliances, tires, and other junk scattered around the overgrown yard. The faded yellow house had a wide front porch and a tall square tower that stuck up above the trees.

They huddled around the locked gate out front. When Mr. Summerling lived here, this gate was never even closed, much less locked. But it was now. Marly dug the little key out of her tote bag and slipped it into the slot at the bottom. The lock clicked open.

"Have either of you ever been inside Mr. Summerling's house?" Sai asked as they started up the front walk.

"No." Isla shook her head.

Marly hadn't been, either. But she'd always wondered what it was like inside. Especially that tower room.

"I wonder what's going to happen to Mr. Summerling's house now that he's . . . *you know* . . ." Isla couldn't say that last word out loud.

Marly remembered how Jay Summerling had asked Ms. Lovelace about the house

in her office that day. Jay had assumed the house was his, but Ms. Lovelace wasn't sure about that. She had other letters from Mr. Summerling, but she refused to open them. She said she had instructions for when each one was to be opened, and she was going to follow those instructions.

"Do you guys think Mr. Summerling is really dead?" Sai asked suddenly.

"What?" Marly asked, shocked.

"Of course he is," Isla said. "That's why Ms. Lovelace read his will."

"I don't know," Sai said as he clomped up the porch stairs. "His body was never found. And think about the treasure hunt we just finished. When would Mr. Summerling have set it all up? Right before he left for this last treasure hunting trip? Why would he do that? He couldn't have known he wasn't ever coming back."

Marly stopped halfway up the steps. She hadn't thought about any of that before.

"Ms. Lovelace probably set it up," Isla said. "Mr. Summerling probably left directions for what to do."

"But when we started the treasure hunt, Ms. Lovelace told us and our parents that she didn't know what was at the end of it, remember?" Marly said. "So how could she have hidden that last note in the tree house?"

"Right?" Sai said, obviously happy to have Marly on his side.

Isla looked a little pale. "Well, where has Mr. Summerling been all this time if he's not dead?"

"Maybe in there." Sai gestured toward the house. "Maybe he's waiting for us to come in right now!"

Isla's face grew even paler as Sai walked over to the door and turned the knob. "It's locked." He frowned.

"Well, I don't think we need a key," Marly said, pressing closer. "See? It's got an electronic keypad. What we need is the combination, like the lock at the tree house."

But unlike the lock at the tree house, this combination required letters, not numbers.

"We could also try ringing the doorbell," Isla said. She pushed the button and a doorbell chimed like a grandfather clock somewhere deep inside the house. They tried

to peer through the front windows, but dark shades blocked their view.

No one came to the door.

"Maybe the combination is hidden in the new letter," Isla suggested. "You know, like the words *make a T* were hidden in that other letter."

Marly pulled the letter out of her bag and they all put their heads together, which knocked Isla's headband to the ground. She bent to pick it up.

"I don't see anything weird with any of the words or letters in this letter," Marly said.

"I can't believe we're stuck already," Sai grumbled. He started pacing back and forth on the porch.

"Wait, that's it!" Isla pointed to the word *stuck* in the new letter. "'If you ever find yourselves—'"

"'—*stuck*,'" Marly read along with her, "'remember who you are. That will always get you through!'"

Sai turned. "Through the door?" He let out a short laugh. "Good one, Mr. S! So, who are we? Sai, Marly, and Isla. But who knows what order he programmed our names?"

"I don't think the combination is our names," Marly said. "Look at the beginning of the letter. 'Dear—'"

"'Treasure Troop,'" Isla said.

"Ah," Sai said. He stepped up to the keypad and pressed T . . . R . . . E . . . A . . . S . . . U . . . R—

It buzzed on the *R* and a red *X* appeared in the corner of the keypad.

"That's not right?" Marly said with surprise.

"Maybe you missed a letter," Isla said. "Try it again."

Sai pressed T . . . R . . . E . . . A . . . S . . . U . . . R—

Bzzzzzt!

"Argh!" Sai stomped his foot. He tried one more time. T . . . R . . . E . . . A . . . S . . . U . . . R—

Bzzzzzt!

"Okay, stop." Marly put her hand on Sai's shoulder. "That's obviously not right."

"Go ahead and try our names," Isla suggested.

Sai tried S . . . A . . . I . . . M . . . A . . . R . . . L—

Bzzzzzt!

And S . . . A . . . I . . . I . . . S . . . L . . . A—

Bzzzzzt!

And I . . . S . . . L . . . A . . . S . . . A . . . I—

Bzzzzzt!

"Wait," Marly said. "It always buzzes after you press a certain number of letters."

"Hey, you're right," Isla said. "How many?" She counted on her fingers while Sai pressed M . . . A . . . R . . . L . . . Y . . . S . . . A—

Bzzzzzt!

"Seven," Sai said. "So, what's a seven-letter word that says what we are?"

"Oh, I know!" Marly said with a grin. "Let me try."

Sai stepped aside and Marly pressed F . . . R . . . I . . . E . . . N . . . D . . . S.

A green check mark appeared on the keypad and the door unlocked.

Chapter 5

MR. SUMMERLING'S HOUSE

"Hello?" Isla called through the open door. "Is anyone here?" One by one, they entered the house.

"I think we're alone," Marly said, closing the door behind them. There was a living room to their right. Heavy red velvet curtains covered the windows, which made the house seem dark. There was a staircase to the second floor on their left. And a long hallway leading to a kitchen stretched in front of them.

"Alone with the ghosts," Sai said, wiggling his fingers eerily.

Isla glared at him.

"What?" Sai said. "That's what the letter says. Right, Marly? One ghost guards the door to the hidden room. Another keeps the key."

"The 'very important key,'" Marly said in a dramatic voice. That line made her smile.

They moved into the dark living room. There was an electric fireplace surrounded by dusty bookshelves against one wall. A deep red sofa by the window. A half-finished Scrabble game on a table in a corner.

Isla flipped a wall switch, but nothing happened.

"Let's try the floor lamp," Marly said. She went over and pulled the chain, but the lamp didn't turn on, either. "Is the electricity out?"

"Kind of looks like it," Isla said.

"Good thing Ms. Lovelace gave us a

flashlight," Sai said, patting the side pocket of
his cargo pants.

"Yeah, good thing," Marly said. Though it
wasn't so dark that they needed a flashlight.
Some sunlight came in around the curtains.
Enough to see by, anyway.

"See any hidden rooms?" Sai asked as
he squeezed past a tall red chair beside the
fireplace. He squinted up at the bookshelf,

then wandered into the next room.

"We should stay together," Isla called after him.

But Sai didn't come back.

Marly sighed. Sai always did things his own way.

The girls followed him into a room that turned out to be a dining room. It was brighter in here. The curtains were made of a faded whitish-yellow lace, which let in a lot more light. There was a table with eight chairs in the middle of the room, a cabinet full of fancy dishes built into one wall, and a map of an island on the wall across from the table.

Marly liked maps, so she went to check it out. There was a cobweb on it. She brushed it away.

The map was hand drawn. In pencil. *Summer Island* it read at the top. *Never heard of it*, Marly thought. There were trees

and hills and a small lake or pond drawn
on the map. *Maybe this is one of the places
Mr. Summerling searched for buried treasure?*

"Hey, check out this weird kitchen," Sai
called from the next room.

Marly looked around and realized that not
only was Sai gone, Isla was, too. She hurried

to catch up with her friends. "Oh, wow," she said, skidding on the black-and-white tile floor. The checkered pattern made her feel sort of dizzy.

But that wasn't the weird part of the kitchen. What was weird was how old-fashioned everything was. Marly had never seen such an old stove or refrigerator before. Not even at her grandma's house.

There were no dishes in the sink. Nothing on the counters. And plain shades covered the windows. It didn't look like anyone had used this kitchen in a while.

There was a door that led to the backyard, and another door beside the refrigerator. Sai opened that one, but it was just a pantry. It held a container of oatmeal and a few canned goods. Not much else.

"Let's see what's upstairs," Sai said. They trooped back down the hallway, rounded a corner, and thudded up the stairs.

They ended up in a hallway with five closed doors.

"Let's see what's behind door number one," Sai said, opening the first door.

"A bedroom," Isla said.

The next room was a bathroom. Then two more bedrooms. And a final door at the end of the hall. Marly tried the handle.

Locked.

But unlike the front door, this one required a key.

"I bet this is our hidden room," Sai said.

"I don't know," Marly said. "It's just locked. It's not hidden."

Sai got down on his hands and knees and tried to peer under the door.

"See anything?" Isla asked.

"No," he said, disappointed.

"Let's take a closer look inside each of the bedrooms," Marly said, turning around. She went inside the yellow one. It didn't have much in it. Just a bed with a white bedspread and a plain brown dresser. There was nothing on the dresser or the walls. Nothing in the closet. Marly had a feeling this room had been used even less recently than the kitchen.

"Isla? Sai?" she called when she returned to the hallway. "Where are you?"

"In here," Isla said, coming out of the bedroom across the hall. "There wasn't anything interesting in there."

Marly craned her neck. That room looked a lot like the one she'd just come from except the walls and dresser were white and the bedspread was blue. As they passed the bathroom again, a small square door on a wall in there caught Marly's eye. She went to check it out. It was just a clothes chute.

"Where'd Sai go?" Marly asked when she rejoined Isla in the hallway.

Isla shrugged. "Maybe he found something in that last bedroom."

The only room Marly and Isla hadn't been in on this floor was the one closest to the stairs. They peeked in and saw it was just as plain as the other two. The walls were green. The bedspread white.

Sai wasn't in there.

"Sai?" Marly called, louder this time. "Where are you?"

No response.

Marly had a bad feeling about this.

Chapter 6

SCRABBLE!

"SAI!" Marly and Isla yelled.

"Down here," Sai called from somewhere downstairs. "I think I found another puzzle."

Marly and Isla glanced at one another, then charged down the stairs.

"Where?" Isla asked. "Where are you?"

"In here."

Marly and Isla followed Sai's voice into the living room and found him hunched over the Scrabble game.

"I don't think this is a real game," he said, staring down at the board. "See? None of the words go over the starting square." He touched the pink square in the middle of the board.

"Also, there aren't any racks of letters on the table," Isla pointed out.

"Maybe the words are another message for us," Marly said. She opened their notebook to a clean page and started copying down all the words on the board: *first, dictionary, the, letter, in, three, scrabble,* and *words*. Then she sat down on the overstuffed sofa and tried to

rearrange the words into a sentence.

"First three two-letter words in the dictionary?" Marly said as Isla and Sai plopped down beside her.

"No. We didn't use the word *Scrabble.*"

Isla twirled her hair around her finger. "Well, there is such a thing as a Scrabble dictionary," she said. "So it could say 'First three two-letter words in the Scrabble dictionary.' Is there a Scrabble dictionary in here?"

Sai hopped over to one of the bookshelves, then tilted his head as he scanned the books.

Isla checked the other shelf. "There *is* one!" she cried, pulling out a hardcover book. "I'm not surprised. Mr. Summerling always liked weird words. And there are lots of weird words in here. Like words that have a *Q*, but no *U.*"

"What?" Marly said. She'd never heard of a word that has a *Q* in it but no *U.*

"We don't care about weird words right now," Sai said, taking the book from Isla. "We care about the first three two-letter words." He flipped back to the beginning of the book.

Marly studied her notebook. "You know? The message could also say 'First two three-letter words in the Scrabble dictionary,'" she said, chewing on the end of her pencil.

"Wait, what was that?" Isla cried.

"What was what?" Marly lifted her head. She didn't hear anything.

But Isla was clearly talking about something she'd seen in the dictionary. Not something she'd heard elsewhere in the house. Isla took the dictionary back and quickly turned the pages until she found what she was looking for.

"Look." She held the book so Marly and Sai could see the small rectangle cut into the pages of the book. Tucked inside the rectangle was a silver key.

"Wow!" Marly's eye opened wide. "That's a great place to hide something!"

"This could be the very important key." Sai grabbed it, accidentally knocking the book from Isla's hands onto the floor. "I bet it unlocks that door at the end of the hall!" He bolted for the stairs.

"Wait, Sai," Isla said, picking up the book. "The whole reason we went looking for a Scrabble dictionary was so we could find the first three two-letter words, remember?"

"Or the first two *three*-letter words," Marly added. "That's what the puzzle was really about. Finding those words. We need to find them and write them down."

Sai groaned and dragged himself back. "I think the whole point of that puzzle was to find this key!"

"There could be two reasons for the puzzle," Isla said. "To find the key *and* look up those words."

Marly agreed. "We may have to enter these words into some other puzzle we haven't found yet," she said. "I think we should look them up before we go off exploring. It won't take long."

Sai exhaled impatiently while Isla turned to the beginning of the book. "Okay, Marly," she said. "The first three two-letter words are—" She frowned. "I don't know how to pronounce them, so I'll just spell them. *A-A, A-B,* and *A-D.*"

Marly copied them into the notebook. "You weren't kidding about weird words," she muttered. "What does *A-A* even mean?"

"It's some kind of lava," Isla said, reading

from the book. "Ready for the first two three-letter words?"

"Sure am."

"*A-A-H* and *A-A-L*," Isla said.

"*More* weird words," Sai said as Marly wrote them down. Isla closed the dictionary and set it on the fireplace mantel.

Marly couldn't disagree. But she was glad they'd taken the time to copy those words into their notebook. Mr. Summerling never gave them a clue without a reason.

"*Now* can we take the very important key and try it in the locked door upstairs?" Sai asked.

"Yep," Marly said, tucking the notebook into her bag.

They dashed for the stairs. But before they were even halfway up, the doorbell rang.

Chapter 7

TROUBLE FROM JAY

They all froze on the stairs.

"Who's that?" Marly asked, gripping the banister.

Whoever it was rang the doorbell again. Then pounded on the door.

"Should we answer it?" Sai asked.

66

"Let's see who it is first," Isla said.

They crept back down the stairs and over to the front door. Marly put her uncovered eye to the peephole.

An angry green eye stared back at her.

Marly gasped. "It's Jay Summerling!"

"I know you kids are in there," Jay growled. "Open this door!" He pounded on it again.

Marly shrank back. Her heart was pounding almost as hard as Jay's fist. "He must not know the code for the lock," she said.

"Good. Let's not open the door," Isla said firmly.

Marly was in total agreement there.

"I'll go make sure the back door is locked," Sai said. "We don't want him to sneak in or anything." He zoomed down the hall.

"You kids are trespassing!" Jay yelled. "Open this door right now or I'll call the police!"

"Go ahead!" Marly couldn't resist yelling back. "We're not trespassing. We're allowed to be here. Are you?"

"Shh!" Isla hissed, grabbing Marly's arm. "Don't talk to him!" Her eyes were wild with fear.

"He already knows we're in here," Marly said. He may have even followed them from Ms. Lovelace's office. Maybe that was why she'd had that creepy feeling that someone was watching them before. Maybe *Jay* had been watching them.

Strangely enough, Marly didn't feel scared. Not too scared, anyway. Not as scared as Isla seemed to be. Maybe that was because she knew her mom was right next door.

"Anything you find in that house is mine, not yours! Do you hear me?" Jay yelled as he pounded some more.

Marly and Isla eyed each other. *What does he think we are going to find in this house?*

Finally, the pounding stopped. Footsteps thudded across the front porch and a shadow passed by the living room window.

"Uh-oh. What if he's going around to the back door?" Marly whispered. She and Isla hadn't moved.

"Hopefully Sai got it locked," Isla whispered back.

But Sai hadn't come back yet.

"Sai?" Marly called in as loud of a voice as she dared. "Where are you? Is the back door locked?"

No response.

"He maybe can't hear us," Isla said.

Marly and Isla inched along the hallway

toward the kitchen. The back door rattled. Then someone pounded on it.

Marly froze. She grabbed Isla's hand. Her heart pulsed in her throat.

But no one came in.

Finally, the pounding stopped and the house went silent.

"Is he gone?" Isla mouthed.

"I don't know," Marly mouthed back. They continued down the hall, their backs pressed against the wall. But when they got to the kitchen, Sai wasn't there.

"Where is he?" Isla said, barely above a whisper.

Marly let go of Isla's hand and took slow, careful steps toward the back door. She pressed her ear to the door. Then, with a shaky finger, she moved the shade just enough to see out onto the back porch and yard.

No one was out there.

"I think Jay's gone," Marly said with relief. "But yeah, where's Sai?"

Marly and Isla grabbed hands again and moved into the dining room. No Sai. Then the living room. Still no Sai.

"Why can't he just stay in one place!" Marly grumbled.

"Because he's Sai," Isla said.

Marly nodded. That was exactly why.

Then Marly noticed the electric fireplace. Strange. The logs were all lit up!

"Isla?" Marly said, staring at the fireplace. "Was the fireplace on when we were in here before?"

Isla turned. She grabbed her hair in her fist. "No," she said, shaking her head. "Who turned it on?"

"Sai?" Marly suggested. She hoped it was Sai. Because if it wasn't him, who else could it have been?

She walked along the fireplace and examined every single brick. "Aha!" she said when she noticed a small switch sticking out between two of the bricks. "I bet this turns it on and off." She flipped the switch and the fireplace went off.

That made her feel better.

But thirty seconds later, the fireplace came on again.

All by itself.

Chapter 8

HELP!

"That was weird," Marly said, not taking her eyes off the fireplace.

Isla reached over and turned it off.

Once again, it popped back on. Then it started blinking: *blinkblinkblink! Blink!* . . . *Blink!* . . . *Blink!* . . . *blinkblinkblink!*

Isla gasped. "I-i-is it a ghost?"

One ghost guards the doors. Another keeps the key. *Are there* really *ghosts in Mr. Summerling's house?* Marly wondered. *Real live ghosts?*

73

Marly wasn't sure she believed in ghosts. But this . . . this was odd. *What is going on here?*

"I don't like this," Isla said, backing away from the fireplace. "Let's find Sai and get out of here." She turned all the way around and headed for the front door.

But Marly couldn't leave. Not yet. *blinkblinkblink! Blink! . . . Blink! . . . Blink! . . . blinkblinkblink!* She narrowed her eyes. "Hey, there's a pattern to the blinking."

Isla turned back around. She squinted, then moved in closer. "You're right. There *is* a

pattern."

blinkblinkblink! Blink! . . . Blink! . . . Blink! . . . blinkblinkblink!

"Short! Short! Short! LONG-LONG-LONG! Short! Short! Short!"

Isla looked at Marly. "That's SOS in Morse code!"

"I don't think a ghost is making that fireplace blink," Marly said.

"It's Sai!" Isla exclaimed. "He's in trouble."

"But where *is* he?" Marly asked. "And how is he making the fireplace blink?"

The last time they'd seen him, he was on his way to lock the back door. Where had he gone after that?

blinkblinkblink! Blink! . . . Blink! . . . Blink! . . . blinkblinkblink!

"Sai?" Isla pounded on the bricks above the fireplace. "Is that you? Can you hear us?" She turned to Marly. "Maybe he found the hidden room. Maybe it's somewhere around here."

Marly had already looked closely at all these bricks. That was how she'd found the switch that turned the fireplace on and off. Was there another switch? Maybe a lever? Maybe even a loose brick?

The girls pushed and pulled at every brick around the fireplace. Every brick they could reach. None seemed loose.

Marly rubbed her eye. She didn't see any other switches or levers, either.

But the fireplace continued to blink: *Short! Short! Short!* LONG-LONG-LONG! *Short! Short! Short!*

"Uh-oh!" Isla said as the fireplace, wall, and floor suddenly began to turn.

"What the—" Marly gaped at the moving floor beneath her feet. Half a second later, she and Isla were thrust into a whole other room.

A dark room.

A flashlight shined in their faces. Marly put a hand up to shield her uncovered eye from the bright light.

"Finally!" Sai said.

"Sai?" Marly and Isla said at the same time.

"Where are we?" Marly blinked. "And please move that flashlight. You're shining it right in my eye."

Sai aimed the flashlight at the gray concrete floor. "We're in a hidden room," he explained.

"*The* hidden room?" Isla asked.

"With the treasure?" Marly said with growing enthusiasm. *Had they found it already?*

"No," Sai said. "I don't think so, anyway. Look around. There's no view of the city. But I'm sure glad we have a flashlight." He shined it all around the bare walls. The room was completely empty.

"What is this room?" Marly turned all around. It wasn't large. Maybe half the size of her bedroom at home. "How did we get in here?"

"I don't know how you guys got in here. But I found a button on the edge of the bookshelf," Sai said.

"Me too!" Isla exclaimed. "It was like a doorbell. And it was stuck to the underside of one of the bookshelves."

"Yes!" Sai said. "After I made sure the back door was locked, I came back through the living room and I saw Jay walking past the window, so I ducked down. That's when I saw the button. I was curious what it did, so I pushed it."

"So did I," Isla admitted.

Marly's eyebrow went up. "You did?" she said. Isla wasn't normally the sort of person who pushed buttons if she didn't know what they did.

Isla cringed a little. "Why didn't you tell us you were in here?" she asked Sai. "Why didn't you answer when we called your name? And why didn't you just come back out?"

"I didn't hear you calling me," Sai said. "Did you hear me calling you?"

"You were calling us?" Marly said.

"Yes! I could sort of see you guys through the fireplace if I got down low. It's a two-sided fireplace. See?" Sai swung the flashlight beam toward the electric log. "I called and pounded on the glass, but you guys didn't answer. This room must be soundproof."

"Weird," Marly said. "Why does Mr. Summerling have a secret soundproof room behind his fireplace?"

"To store his treasure?" Isla suggested.

"But there isn't any treasure in here. There isn't anything in here," Sai said. "Not even a button to get us out of here."

"What!" Isla exclaimed at the same time Marly said, "There's no button on this side of the wall?"

Sai shook his head. "The only button I've found is the one that turns the fireplace on and off. That's why I started flashing SOS. It was all I had. I was hoping you'd see that and find me."

"There has to be another button in here somewhere," Marly said, feeling along the concrete wall.

"I don't think there is," Sai said. "And you have to be standing right up by the fireplace when someone pushes the button. See? This is the part of the floor that moves." He shined the flashlight onto a half circle in front of the fireplace. There was a small gap between it and the rest of the floor.

Isla stepped onto it. "So, what do we do?" she asked. "Stand here until someone comes along and pushes the button and lets us out?"

Sai snorted. "When's *that* going to happen?" he asked. "We locked all the doors, remember? And even if someone did come in, who knows about that button? Who else even knows about this hidden room?"

"Too bad none of us have cell phones," Marly grumbled, resting her shoulder against the wall. "If we did, we could call someone to come let us out."

But none of their parents wanted them to have cell phones until they were in middle school.

"There's probably no service in here anyway," Isla said. She stared at the floor. "I should never have pushed that button. What are we going to do?"

Chapter 9

SECRET STAIRS

"There has to be a way out of here," Marly said, looking around. But it was hard to see in the dark. "Shine that flashlight around, Sai."

"I have. Believe me, I have," Sai said in a tired voice. But he shined the flashlight up and down and all around the room.

Marly crossed her arms. "Mr. Summerling lived here alone," she reminded everyone. "How did he get out of here if the only button is on the other side of this room?"

"Good question," Isla said. "We need to check every inch of this place." She and Marly moved side by side along the wall. The concrete scratched their fingers as they felt up and down.

Sai tried to light their way with the flashlight, but Marly still nearly tripped over something on the floor.

"Careful," Isla said, grabbing Marly's arm before she fell. "Are you okay?"

"Yeah," Marly said, regaining her footing. "What is that?" She kicked at a metal plate that stuck up out of the floor.

Sai shined the flashlight on it. It was a rust-colored square, a bit bigger than the size of the hopscotch squares at school. It had a handle on it.

Marly tugged at the handle and was surprised to discover how easily it came up.

"A door!" Isla exhaled in relief. And beneath the door was a set of stairs that disappeared

into darkness. They peered over the edge.

"Well, what are we waiting for?" Sai walked around the opening and stepped onto the top stair. While Marly and Isla climbed in carefully behind him, Sai moved down a couple of steps and tried to shine the flashlight the rest of the way down. It didn't illuminate much.

"Should we close the door behind us?" Isla asked, holding onto a wall for balance.

"Yeah, let's," Marly said. She reached up, and she and Isla gently pulled the door over their heads while Sai held the flashlight so they could see what they were doing.

"Hey, there's a lock on this side of the door," Sai said, aiming the flashlight at it. He climbed back up, squeezed in between Marly and Isla, and slid the lock into place.

"I don't know if that's a good idea," Marly said.

"Why not?" Sai asked. "We can always unlock it."

"Not if we get stuck in there again." Marly banged her hand on the door above them.

"That's not going to happen," Sai said. "We know how we got in there. I'm not pressing that button again anytime soon."

"Neither am I," Isla said.

Marly felt a little jealous that Isla and Sai had both found some button—an *important* button that she never saw. *My stupid eyes,* she thought as she followed Sai down the rest of the stairs and into a narrow tunnel.

"Well, let's see where this goes," Sai said, his voice echoing against the narrow walls.

Isla put her hands on Marly's shoulders, who then put her hands on Sai's. Slowly, they snaked their way through the tunnel with Sai lighting the path ahead.

"Can you imagine being down here without a flashlight?" Isla asked. Her mouth was inches from Marly's ear.

"Let's not imagine. Let's see!" Sai switched

the flashlight off and everything went black.

"SAI!" the girls cried.

Marly slapped his arm and Sai turned the flashlight back on. "Just kidding," he said. They pressed on, their hands back on one another's shoulders.

"I wonder what this tunnel is for," Isla said. "There's nothing down here."

"Maybe it's a secret passageway to the hidden room," Sai said.

"We just came from a hidden room," Marly said.

"Yeah, but that one didn't look out over the city, so there must be another one," Sai said.

"We're in a basement," Isla said. "No room down here is going to look out over the city."

"But we're about to go up," Sai said. "See?" He shined the flashlight on a metal spiral stairway.

"Sai could be right. This tunnel might be a secret passageway to the room we're looking for," Marly said excitedly as they began climbing the stairs.

But the stairs went on and on and on. Round and round and round.

"We must be going all the way to the third floor." Sai stopped to catch his breath.

"There isn't a third floor," Marly said.

Sai glanced over his shoulder. "Are you sure?"

Marly thought for a second. They hadn't found any stairs leading to a third floor when they were on the second floor. But there was definitely a tower on Mr. Summerling's house. Where was it? How did you get to it?

"Well . . ." Okay, Marly *wasn't* sure there wasn't a third floor. When it came to Mr. Summerling, she wasn't sure of much of anything.

They continued up, up, up the stairs. As they climbed, the beam from the flashlight bounced all around.

"Wh-what's that?" Isla asked, clinging to Marly's arm.

Marly held tight to the railing. "What's what?" She peered into the darkness. She could almost feel Isla's heart beating through her arm, but she had no idea what Isla was talking about.

Isla loosened her grip. "I-I don't know," she stammered. "For a second there, I thought I saw a-a ghost."

"Hello?" Sai called, shining the flashlight all around the stairwell.

"There it is again!" Isla pointed.

The flashlight beam swept slowly back and forth, finally landing on a painting on the wall. A painting of an angry ghost lady.

"Huh." Sai took two more steps, then stopped in front of the painting. "This is a strange place to hang a painting."

Marly and Isla gathered around him on the stairs.

Isla wrinkled her nose. "It's creepy."

"Maybe that's why it's in here," Marly said. "So no one has to look at it."

"We're almost to the top." Sai aimed the flashlight at a closed door above them. "Let's keep going."

"I bet that door's going to be locked," Isla said.

"We've got a key, remember?" Sai said, patting his front pocket. "The very important key from the dictionary?" He hurried up the rest of the stairs. "But guess what?" He turned to the girls. "We don't need it." He opened the door and they were back on the second floor of the house.

"Hey, this is the door we couldn't get in before," Isla said as it closed behind them.

Marly reached over and tried the handle. Locked again. "And now we can't get back in," she said.

Chapter 10

THE KEY TO...?

"Maybe we can," Sai said. "Hold this." He handed Marly the flashlight, then stuck his hand in his front pocket and pulled out the key from the dictionary. Then he inserted the key into the lock and turned the knob. "Voilà!" he said as the door opened.

"Well, okay then," Marly said, pleased that something was finally going their way.

Sai held the door open for a few seconds, then let it drift closed.

"It's nice that we know what to do with that

key, but I still feel like we're back where we started," Isla said, leaning against the wall "Sure, we found a hidden room, but there's no treasure in there and it doesn't look out over the city. We have a key, but I wouldn't say it was kept by a ghost. We have a list of two-letter words and three-letter words from the Scrabble dictionary, but we have no idea what to do with them. Are we even on the right track?"

"I wouldn't say we're back where we started," Marly said, though she understood Isla's frustration. "That's all stuff we've found. We just don't know how it fits together." She turned the flashlight off.

"Why don't we go downstairs and see if we can figure it out," Sai said. He took the flashlight from Marly and shoved the key back inside his front pocket.

"All right," Isla said, and they headed back down the hall.

Marly paused at the top of the stairs. "Wow. Look at that," she said, gazing up at a huge painting on the wall in front of her.

There was an old-fashioned girl in a blue dress in the painting. She was admiring her reflection in a floor-length mirror. There was also a *ghost* in the painting. A ghost girl who had no reflection. The ghost girl hovered between the other girl and the mirror. She didn't seem to be looking at the girl. She was looking out at Marly, Isla, and Sai.

"Mr. Summerling sure likes paintings of ghosts, doesn't he?" Isla said, twisting her hair around her finger.

"He does," Sai agreed. "But look at what that ghost is looking at."

"You mean us?" Marly asked.

"Uh-uh." Sai shook his head. "She's looking at the door we just came out of. It's almost like she's *guarding* that door." He pointed at it.

Marly took a step toward the painting. "You

know? You're right," she said, glancing back and forth between it and the door. "Maybe Mr. Summerling wasn't talking about real ghosts when he wrote 'One ghost guards the doors. Another keeps the key.' Maybe he was talking about ghosts in *paintings*."

"This one is guarding a door," Sai said. "Maybe the one in there," he pointed at the locked door again, "is guarding the very important key."

"But we already have the very important key," Isla said.

"We have *a* key," Marly said. "Maybe there's *another* key hidden somewhere around that other painting. Maybe that's the 'very important' one." *There had to be a reason Mr. Summerling added that part.*

"And maybe that's the key that leads to the treasure that's in a hidden room that looks out over the city," Sai added. "*Not* the hidden room behind the fireplace."

"Let's see if there's another key," Marly said.

They raced back down the hall.

"I guess that would explain why there's a painting in there where no one can see it," Isla said as Sai unlocked the door and turned on the flashlight.

They stepped back inside the hidden stairwell and let the door close behind them.

"I sure wish that door would stay open," Isla said with a nervous glance over her shoulder.

"It's not a big deal," Marly said as they descended the stairs. "The door opens from this side."

"I know," Isla said. "But I still wish it would stay open."

"Here we are," Sai said, stopping beside the creepy painting. He shined the flashlight on it and felt around the frame.

Marly felt along the other side of the frame. All of a sudden, her fingers brushed against a small latch. She squeezed it and the painting swung open like a door.

"Oh!" Isla said, staring at something on the wall behind the painting.

Marly ducked under the painting so she could see what Isla was looking at. "It's a safe," she said.

Sai tried the handle, but it didn't open.

"Look at the lock," Isla said, pointing at six dials. Each one had a bunch of letters on it. "I think we can figure out the combination." She grinned at Marly.

Sai looked confused. "How?"

"Don't you remember?" Marly reached into her tote bag for their notebook. "'First three two-letter words in the Scrabble dictionary' or 'first two three-letter words in the Scrabble dictionary'?"

"Ohhh, yeah," Sai said with a grin.

Marly flipped pages in the notebook until she found where she'd copied down those

words. "Try A-A-A-B-A-D," she said.

Sai held the flashlight while Isla spun each dial to the correct letter. There was a kerchunking sound of metal on metal when Isla tried the door.

Still locked.

"Okay, let's try the three letter words. A-A-H-A-A-L," Marly said.

Isla spun the dials again. This time the door clicked open. She squealed and reached inside. "Yes!" she cried, pulling out a shiny silver key. "*This* must be the 'very important key.'"

"Okay, but where do we use it?" Sai asked.

"On the other hidden room," Marly said. "The one that looks out over the city."

But where is that?

They closed the safe and carefully moved the painting back in front of it. Then they tromped back up the stairs and out to the second floor. As the door to the hidden stairway closed behind them, the ghost in the other painting stared straight at them.

Isla's brow furrowed. "Can I see that letter from Mr. Summerling again?" she asked Marly.

"Sure." Marly dug in her bag and handed it to Isla. "What are you looking for?" She watched Isla's eyes scan the paper.

"This," Isla said finally. "'One ghost guards the *doors.*'" She touched the word for extra emphasis, then pointed at the painting in front of them. "That ghost is definitely guarding the door to the secret stairs. But could she be guarding *another* door, too?"

Marly looked around. She didn't see any other doors they hadn't already checked out.

Sai hurried toward the painting. "Maybe it's like that other painting. Maybe there's a door behind it," he said, tugging on the frame.

It didn't move.

But it was a much larger painting than the other one. *Probably heavier, too*, Marly thought. "Here, let me help," she said. She put her hands above Sai's. Isla put her hands below.

"One, two, three, pull!" Marly said.

The painting still didn't budge.

"Let's try the other side," Isla said. They lined up on the other side of the frame, found their grips, and pulled again.

This time, the painting creaked open. And revealed a hidden door!

Marly bounced on her toes and giggled in delight.

"I knew it!" Sai said, rubbing his hands together.

It was smaller than a regular door, but not quite as small as the door to the tree house. Marly tried the door. It was, of course, locked.

"Could *this* be 'the very important key'?" Isla asked, holding up the new key. She inserted it into the lock and turned the handle.

The door opened.

"Yes!" Sai said. They all high-fived.

Another set of stairs beckoned. Daylight poured down the stairs.

"I bet the hidden room that looks out over the city is right up there!" Marly bent and tried to see what was up the stairs, but she couldn't. Not from this angle.

"Let's go," Sai said, giving her a light push.
But as Marly's foot touched the bottom
step, they heard glass breaking downstairs.

Chapter 11

CAUGHT!

"What was that?" Isla asked, grabbing onto her hair.

More glass shattered. Then heavy footsteps.

"We aren't alone anymore," Marly whispered. "Quick! Let's close this back up." She pulled the door closed, and Isla and Sai helped her move the painting back in front of it.

"Where are you kids? I know you're in here!" Someone with a gruff voice tromped around downstairs.

Sai flattened himself against the wall. "I-is

that . . . Jay?" he asked, his voice shaking.

"I think so." Marly gulped. *And it sounds like he is in the house!*

"What are we going to do?" Isla whispered.

Marly racked her brain. "The hidden stairway!" she said. "We can hide in there."

"I want to know what you're doing in my house!" Jay shouted.

"It's not your house!" Sai shouted back as Marly and Isla gaped at him.

"What are you doing?" Marly hissed.

Sai gave Marly a sheepish look. "It's not," he mouthed.

Not the point, Marly thought. "Open the door!" She elbowed Sai. He was the one who had the key.

"It *is* my house," Jay said. "And you three are trespassing!"

"Hurry!" Isla pulled on Sai's arm.

But Sai didn't unlock the door. "You're the one who's trespassing," he yelled at Jay. He stormed down the hallway. *And* down the stairs. "We were invited. Were you?"

Marly and Isla raised their hands in helpless frustration. They didn't have a key to the hidden stairway. What else could they do but reluctantly follow Sai?

Downstairs, the large window behind the sofa had been shattered. Broken glass littered the sofa, table, and floor. And Jay Summerling, dressed in a suit and tie, stood beside the overturned Scrabble game with his hands on his hips.

Sai bent to pick up a baseball-size rock. *So that's how he got in here.*

"Doesn't look like you were invited," Marly said. Isla hovered behind her.

"Yeah, this is

Mr. Summerling's house, not yours," Sai said. "He left you out of his will, remember? He left all his treasure to *us*!"

"So, there *is* treasure," Jay said greedily. "What is it? *Where* is it?" He eyeballed each of them in turn.

Marly pressed her lips together. They all remained silent.

"TELL ME!" he screamed, his angry voice shooting right through Marly. Isla reached for Marly's hand.

Jay stood tall, took a deep breath, and lowered his voice. "If you don't tell me where it is, I'll call the police." He reached into his pocket and pulled out a cell phone. "I'll tell them you all broke into my dad's house and I caught you trying to steal from him."

"You're the one who broke in!" Isla argued.

Jay's smile was pure evil. "I don't think the police will see it that way. I'm an upstanding businessman. You are children.

Who do you think they'll believe?"

"Us!" Marly said, summoning courage she didn't know she had. "Because Ms. Lovelace will tell the police she gave us this letter." She patted the tote bag that hung from her shoulder. "We're on another treasure hunt, and we can show the police how we got in here. We didn't have to break a window to get in like you did."

"Unfortunately, Stella Lovelace is gone," Jay said.

"What do you mean *gone*?" Sai asked. He shifted the rock from one hand to the other.

"She's not gone," Isla said. "We were just in her office a couple hours ago."

"Oh, I know." Jay moved toward them. "I saw you from my own office down the street. I wanted to know what you were up to, so when you left her office, I watched you. Then I followed you. I waited while you went inside the house next door, and then I watched you go in here. I rang the bell. When you didn't answer, I went back to Ms. Lovelace's office to find out what was going on. But her office was all locked up. There was a note on the window that says, 'Out for the rest of the summer.'"

"What?" Isla said, confused.

"Out where?" Marly asked. Why would Ms. Lovelace have suddenly closed up her office in two hours? It didn't make any sense.

"I don't know," Jay said. "And her phone goes right to voice mail. Speaking of phones . . ." He raised his phone. "Are you going to show me the treasure or am I going to call the police?"

Marly, Isla and Sai exchanged nervous looks. They hadn't actually found the treasure yet. It was *probably* in that hidden room behind the painting upstairs, but they weren't absolutely certain of it. Either way, they sure didn't want Jay Summerling tagging along while they found out. And they were pretty sure Mr. Summerling wouldn't have wanted that, either.

"Fine. We'll show you where the treasure is," Isla said finally.

Marly gaped at Isla. *Is she out of her mind?*

"Oh, no, we won't!" Sai argued, blocking the entrance to the hallway and stairs.

Isla got right up in Sai's face and said, "We

don't want him to call the police." Then, ever so slightly, she tilted her head toward the fireplace. "I bet you didn't know there's a hidden room behind the fireplace," she said to Jay.

Ah. *Now* Marly knew what Isla was up to. Isla was so smart!

Curiously, Jay walked over to the fireplace. He scanned the mantel and touched all the bricks. Just like Marly and Isla had done. "How do you get in there?" he asked. He stood with one foot on the marble half circle in front of the fireplace and one foot off.

Isla pointed. "You have to have both feet on the marble."

Jay narrowed his eyes. "What are you trying to pull?" He still had one foot on the marble and one foot off.

"No, Isla! Don't tell him. We don't want him to know where the treasure is," Marly said. She hoped she sounded convincing. She hoped Jay would think there was treasure hidden behind the fireplace.

"That's right," Sai said, walking over to Jay. "It's our treasure. Not his!"

Jay shoved him out of the way, then stepped back onto the marble. This time with both feet. "How do you get in there?" he asked Isla.

"Like this!" Isla lunged for the underside of a shelf by the fireplace and jabbed something with the palm of her hand. The whole fireplace wall immediately swung around, taking Jay with it.

"So cool!" Sai breathed.

The fireplace wall that faced them now looked exactly like the other one. You'd never know anything had changed. Or that there was a hidden room behind that fireplace.

"Good thinking, Isla!" Marly patted her friend on the back.

Isla beamed.

"I'm glad we locked the metal door in there that leads to the hidden stairway," Sai said.

Marly nodded. She was glad they'd done that now, too.

"I meant it when I said we don't want *him* to call the police," Isla said. "But *we* should call them. Should we go over to your house and do that?" She looked at Marly.

"Not yet," Sai said. "Jay isn't going anywhere. So let's go back upstairs and see what's in that room behind the painting first."

113

Chapter 12

REMEMBER THE TREE HOUSE

The kids raced back up the stairs. Quickly, they pulled the painting away from the wall and unlocked the hidden door. Then they grabbed hands and clomped up this brand-new set of stairs.

"Oh, wow," Marly said as they entered a small, square room with windows all around. It was the tower room!

"This is it," Isla said, rushing to one of the windows. "The hidden room that looks out over the city." The whole town of Sandford lay

below them, looking small from this height.

"So, where's the treasure?" Sai looked around. There wasn't much in here. Just a couple of boxes beside the stairs and an overstuffed green chair by one of the windows.

Sai crouched down in front of one of the

boxes and searched through it. "Just old clothes in here," he said.

Marly checked the next box. "Looks like photo albums in this box," she said. She took the top album out. "Maybe our next clue is in one of the photos." As she sat down with the album, something on the wall caught her eye: a picture of a telephone.

She quickly stood back up. "Uh, you guys?" she said, turning in a slow circle. There were also pictures of a bear and a globe and a vase of daisies on the walls. "Where else have we seen pictures of a telephone, a bear, a globe, and daisies?"

"The tree house!" Isla and Sai exclaimed.

"That can't be a coincidence," Isla said.

Marly agreed. There had to be a reason Mr. Summerling had the same pictures on the walls in the tree house *and* in this hidden room. She moved to the center of the room. "I don't think the treasure is in the boxes," she said.

"I bet it's like the tree house," Sai said. "We have to figure out where imaginary lines between all the pictures make a T, and that's where we'll find the treasure!"

Marly was already standing on that spot. But unlike in the tree house, there was no rug beneath her feet here. Just plain wood slats.

They all knelt down and pushed their fingers into the gaps between the slats.

"Here we go," Isla said as she lifted the first piece of wood from the floor. There was something metal and blue tucked in there.

"Another secret compartment!" Sai cried. He pulled two more boards up, then Isla lifted the box out and set it on the floor between her and Marly. It was identical to the other two boxes they'd found on the first treasure hunt.

Sai was practically bursting with excitement. "What's in there?" he asked, rubbing his hands together.

Isla unlocked the clips and lifted the lid. A

brown envelope lay inside the box.

Marly grabbed it and tore it open. Inside was a folded sheet of paper *From the Desk of Harry P. Summerling*, three plane tickets to Seattle, Washington, and three tickets to Summer Island. "What the—?" she said, holding them up.

"Where's Summer Island?" Sai asked.

"Probably near Seattle?" Marly guessed.

"There's a map of it in the dining room."

"Those tickets are for *us*," Isla said. "They have our names on them."

"And they're dated August 25," Marly pointed out. "That must be why the letter Ms. Lovelace gave us said we had until August 25 or the treasure would be lost forever. These tickets will probably expire if we don't use them." She waved the tickets in the air.

"Read the letter!" Isla nudged Marly.

Marly unfolded it, and Isla and Sai leaned in while she read it out loud. "'Dear Treasure Troop. Congratulations! You are one step closer to the buried treasure. Please call Stella Lovelace on her private phone (219-555-0155). She will be your guide on your next adventure. Pack your digging clothes. And whatever you do, don't let my son know where you're going. Sincerely, Harry P. Summerling.'"

"So . . . that's our treasure?" Sai said. "A trip to a place called Summer Island?" Marly couldn't tell if he was happy or disappointed.

But Isla's feelings were clear. "I've never been on a plane before," she said with delight.

"I've only been on one once," Marly said.

Finally, Sai leaped to his feet. "We're going on a trip! We're going on a trip!" he said, jumping up and down.

"I wonder what we're going to do on Summer Island," Marly said.

"Duh," Sai said. "We're probably going to go on another treasure hunt!"

Another treasure hunt, Marly thought. *Really?*

"You'll be hearing from my attorney," Jay Summerling grumbled. His hands were handcuffed behind his back.

"Yeah, yeah," the police officer said as she pushed Jay's head down and helped him into a squad car. Then they drove away.

Marly, Isla, Sai, and all of their parents stood around on the sidewalk.

"We should never have let you all go into

that house by yourselves," Isla's mom said as she bounced the baby in her arms.

"Yes, you should have," Sai argued. "We caught a bad guy!"

"And we found the treasure," Marly said, holding up the envelope they'd discovered hidden in the floor.

"Right. Now, what's this about a trip?" Marly's mom asked.

Marly handed the envelope over. Her mom opened it while the other parents moved in closer to see what was inside.

"Before you say anything, can we just call Ms. Lovelace?" Sai asked. "Please?"

"That sounds like a good idea," Marly's mom said, passing the tickets to the other parents. "We need to see what this is all about."

They all went over to Marly's house and sat down on the front porch. Marly's mom pulled out her phone and punched in Ms. Lovelace's number. Then she put her phone on speaker and set it down where everyone could hear it.

"Hello?" Ms. Lovelace said.

"Hi! It's us! Marly, Isla, and Sai! The Treasure Troop!" They all spoke over one another.

Ms. Lovelace laughed. "Well, hello, Treasure Troop! Are you ready for your next adventure?"

"Yes!" they shouted.

"Wait a minute." Sai's dad rested a hand on Sai's shoulder. "What do you mean by '*next* adventure'? How many adventures and treasure hunts are there?"

"I've been wondering the same thing," Isla's mom said with some concern. "Our children have already been on two treasure hunts. How many more are there?"

Marly's excitement fizzled just a bit. Were the parents going to say no to this trip? They couldn't do that. They couldn't!

"I can't answer that," Ms. Lovelace said.

"But you must allow your children to come on this next one. Please! It's the most important one yet!"

The most important one yet? Marly, Isla, and Sai eyed each other curiously. What did *that* mean?

Marly couldn't wait to find out!

THE END